JUST SO THANKFUL

BY MERCER MAYER

For Justinie-Weenie McNair

■ HarperFestival®

A Division of HarperCollins*Publishers*

Library of Congress catalog card number: 2006920320
A Big Tuna Trading Company, LLC/J. R. Sansevere Book
www.harpercollinschildrens.com   www.littlecritter.com
2 3 4 5 6 7
❖
First Edition

Today Mom took Little Sister and me to the toy store.

I wanted to buy this cool scooter called the Super
Streak, but my piggy bank didn't have enough money.
"Why don't you pick something else," said Mom.
But I only wanted the Super Streak. It was so unfair.

Little Sister asked if I wanted to play tea party with her new tea set. But I told her to leave me alone, because I was still so mad. Mom said she didn't know why I was mad, because I have lots of other toys.

"There will always be things you want but don't have, Little Critter," she said. "What's important is appreciating what you do have, like a family that loves you."

On our way home, we saw a boy moving into the biggest house in our whole neighborhood. And guess what he was riding?

The Super Streak! He had the most toys I'd ever seen in my whole life.

I wish I had so many toys.

The new boy didn't take the bus to school like my friends and me. He got driven in a limousine.

He told us his name was Holden Harrison III, but that we could call him H. H. Then he showed us his cell phone. He's the only kid in school with his very own phone and a name that's just two letters.

"Wow, H. H.!" I said. "You are so lucky."

H. H. invited my friends and me to come to his house for a sleepover. We went swimming in his gigantic pool . . .

. . . and we watched a movie on this great big TV. We made a mess with the popcorn and the candy and the sodas, but the maid said it was okay. She cleaned everything up.

And in the morning there was this big breakfast just for us.
"Wow, H. H.!" I said. "You are so lucky! You get the
prize in every cereal box since you don't have to share
with anybody."

On the way home, I told Mom about all the fun stuff we did at H. H.'s house.

"Why don't you invite H. H. to our house," Mom asked.

"But he might get bored, since we don't have so much cool stuff to play with," I said.

Mom just smiled and told me to invite him anyway.

When H. H. came over, we played football. The dog chewed up one of his new sneakers and got mud all over him, but he didn't care. He said he had always wanted a dog.

I told Little Sister not to bug us, but H. H. said it
was okay. He even played tea party with her and Kitty.
And he let her win at checkers, too.

When it was time for dinner, he helped me set the table even though it was my chore.

And then he helped Dad barbecue the hamburgers. H. H. said he never gets to help with dinner at his house.

He didn't even mind when Grandma and Grandpa asked him tons of questions and when Grandma patted him on the head. He said he never sees his grandparents because they live so far away.

When it was time for H. H. to go, our
whole family went outside to say good-bye.
"You're so lucky, Little Critter," H. H. said.

I wondered what he meant, but then I looked around at my family, and all of a sudden I knew.

Maybe I didn't have a Super Streak or a big, fancy house and a maid to pick up my stuff. But what I did have was the best family in the whole world.

"Thank you, everybody!" I yelled. Then I gave them all a great big hug!